Note to parents, carers and teachers

Read it yourself is a series of modern stories, favourite characters and traditional tales written in a simple way for children who are learning to read. The books can be read independently or as part of a guided reading session.

Each book is carefully structured to include many high-frequency words vital for first reading. The sentences on each page are supported closely by pictures to help with understanding, and to offer lively details to talk about.

The books are graded into four levels that progressively introduce wider vocabulary and longer stories as a reader's ability and confidence grows.

Ideas for use

- Begin by looking through the book and talking about the pictures. Has your child heard this story before?

- Help your child with any words he does not know, either by helping him to sound them out or supplying them yourself.

- Developing readers can be concentrating so hard on the words that they sometimes don't fully grasp the meaning of what they're reading. Answering the puzzle questions on pages 30 and 31 will help with understanding.

For more information and advice on Read it yourself and book banding, visit www.ladybird.com/readityourself

Book Band
5

Level 2 is ideal for children who have received some reading instruction and can read short, simple sentences with help.

Special features:

Frequent repetition of main story words and phrases

Short, simple sentences

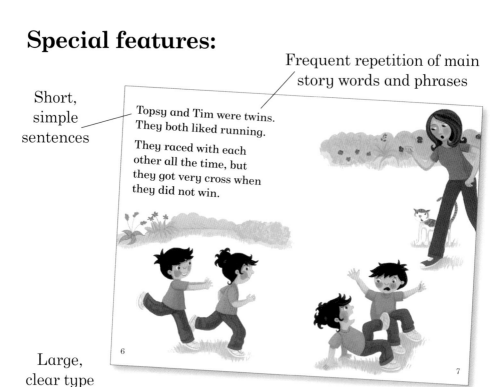

Topsy and Tim were twins. They both liked running.

They raced with each other all the time, but they got very cross when they did not win.

6

7

Large, clear type

Careful match between story and pictures

One day, it was sports day at school.

Mummy came to school with Topsy and Tim to see the twins race.

8

9

Educational Consultant: Geraldine Taylor
Book Banding Consultant: Kate Ruttle

Written by Lorraine Horsley
Illustrated by Belinda Worsley

A catalogue record for this book is available from the British Library

Published by Ladybird Books Ltd
80 Strand, London, WC2R 0RL
A Penguin Company

001

ISBN: 978-0-72327-385-1

Printed in China

Topsy and Tim

The Big Race

By Jean and Gareth Adamson

Topsy and Tim were twins. They both liked running.

They raced with each other all the time, but they got very cross when they did not win.

One day, it was sports day at school.

Mummy came to school with Topsy and Tim to see the twins race.

"Tim, I can run faster than you," said Topsy. "I will win all of the sports day races."

"No, you will not!" said Tim. "Yes, I will!" said Topsy.

The first sports day race was the running race.

Topsy and Tim both ran as fast as they could, but they did not win.

They were both very cross.

The next race was the obstacle race. Hoops were one of the obstacles.

"I will win the obstacle race," said Topsy.

"No, you will not! I will win!" said Tim.

15

But Topsy and Tim got stuck in the hoop together and they did not win the obstacle race.

They were both very cross.

17

The next race was the
sack race.

Topsy and Tim both
got stuck in the sacks.
They did not win
the sack race and
they were both
very cross.

The next race was the dressing-up race. They each had to put umbrellas up.

Topsy and Tim liked dressing up but they could not put the umbrellas up. They did not win the race and they were both very cross.

Next was the egg and spoon race. This race was just for mums.

Topsy and Tim's mummy ran as fast as she could with the egg and spoon – and she came first!

Topsy and Tim had to run together for the next race.

"We will win this race, just you see," they said.

Topsy and Tim ran as fast as they could. This time, they came first!

And this time, they were not cross!

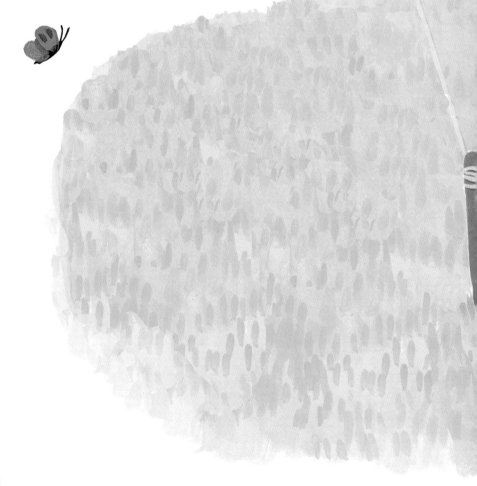

"See, twins!" said Mummy.
"You run faster at sports day
when you run together!"

How much do you remember about the story of Topsy and Tim: The Big Race? Answer these questions and find out!

- Who comes to Sports Day to watch Topsy and Tim?

- What do Topsy and Tim get stuck in during the obstacle race?

- What do Topsy and Tim get stuck in during the sack race?

- Where does Mummy come in the egg and spoon race?

Look at the pictures and match them to the story words.

Topsy

Tim

Mummy

hoops

sacks

umbrellas

Read it yourself with Ladybird

Tick the books you've read!

For beginner readers who can read short, simple sentences with help.

Level 2

☐ ☐

☐ ☐ ☐ ☐ ☐ ☐ ☐

☐ ☐ ☐ ☐ ☐ ☐ ☐

For more confident readers who can read simple stories with help.

Level 3

☐ ☐

☐ ☐ ☐ ☐ ☐ ☐ ☐

The Read it yourself with Ladybird app is now available for iPad, iPhone and iPod touch

App also available on Android devices